PUMPKINS

A Story for a Field

WRITTEN BY

Mary Lyn Ray

ILLUSTRATED BY BARRY ROOT

A Gulliver Green Book

Harcourt Brace & Company

San Diego   New York   London

Requests for permission to make copies of any part of the
work should be mailed to: Permissions Department,
Harcourt Brace & Company,
6277 Sea Harbor Drive, Orlando, Florida 32887-6777.
Gulliver Green is a registered trademark
of Harcourt Brace & Company.

Library of Congress Cataloging-in-Publication Data
Ray, Mary Lyn.
Pumpkins: A Story for a Field/written by Mary Lyn Ray;
illustrated by Barry Root.
— 1st ed.

p.   cm.
"A Gulliver Green book"
Summary: A man harvests and sells a bountiful crop of pumpkins
so that he will be able to preserve a field from developers.
ISBN 0-15-252252-2
[1. Conservation of natural resources — Fiction.
2. Conservationists — Fiction. 3. Pumpkins — Fiction.]
I. Root, Barry, ill. II. Title.
PZ7.R210154Pu   1992
[E] — dc20   90-47305

C D E F G

Printed in Singapore

Gulliver Green® Books focus on various aspects of ecology and
the environment, and a portion of the proceeds from the
sale of these books will be donated to protect,
preserve, and restore native forests.

The illustrations in this book were done in watercolor and
gouache on D'Arches 140 lb. hot-press watercolor paper.
The display type was set in Gallia.
The text type was set in Cloister Oldstyle.
Composition by Thompson Type, San Diego, California
Color separations were made by Bright Arts, Ltd., Singapore.
Printed and bound by Tien Wah Press, Singapore
Production supervision by Warren Wallerstein and Cheryl Kennedy
Designed by Michael Farmer

For all who believe enough

— M L R

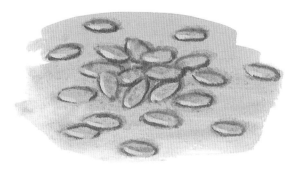

For Kim

— B R

ONCE UPON A TIME there was a field. It was a
particular field in a particular place, where it lived among
young hills that would grow up to be mountains.

Across from this field there lived a man who loved it.

One day a sign appeared in the field. It said For Sale.

The man knew what that meant. Bulldozers, houses, streets and streetlights. The man cried.

He wished he could buy the field. Then it could
always stay a field. But he had very little money. He
counted what he had, and it wasn't enough.

So the man sold his furniture and his paintings and his
silverware and his pocket watch. He sold everything he
owned except his bed and his stove and his bathtub.
Still he didn't have enough.
What could he do?

The man talked to the field, and the field said it would help.

They considered growing Christmas trees, which the man could sell in the city. But trees grow slowly. There wasn't time.

They considered growing cows. But they would need a barn and milk pails, which they didn't have.

Then the man thought of pumpkins.

The next day he went to the farm store and bought an envelope of seeds, which he scattered in the field.

The rain came and wet them, the sun came and warmed them, and they grew. Soon the field was covered in pumpkins. And they grew and they grew and they grew.

When it was time to harvest, there were four hundred sixty-one thousand, two hundred and twelve pumpkins, which the man planned to sell for a dollar each. That would be enough.

He rented fourteen hundred trucks, thirty-seven
boats and eight hundred airplanes to carry them away.
A rug merchant lent him a hundred flying carpets for
the rest.

The man got an atlas and looked up all the kings of all the countries. Then he telephoned them and told them he was shipping them some pumpkins. Where there were democracies, he called the congresses.

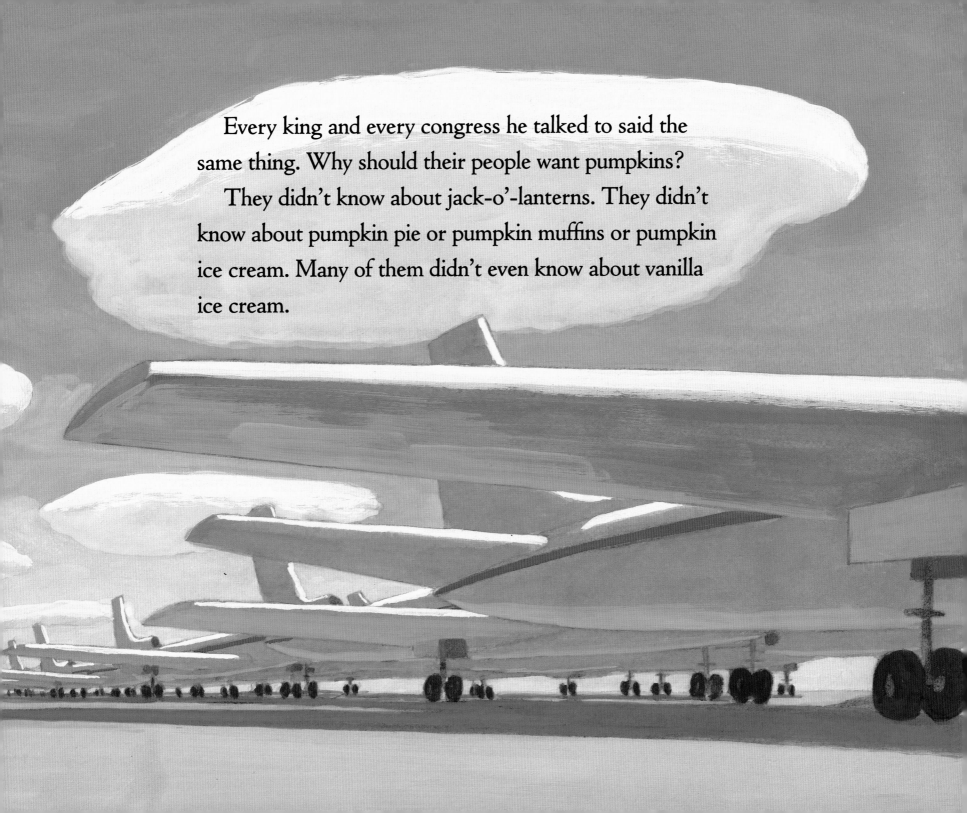

Every king and every congress he talked to said the
same thing. Why should their people want pumpkins?
They didn't know about jack-o'-lanterns. They didn't
know about pumpkin pie or pumpkin muffins or pumpkin
ice cream. Many of them didn't even know about vanilla
ice cream.

So the man wrote four hundred sixty-one thousand, two hundred and twelve tags to tie to his pumpkins to explain what they were for. Luckily he knew how to write in many languages.

Then he sent the pumpkins out.

When they arrived — these round, orange, heavy, bumpy pumpkins — people read the tags and bought them. In Dundee, West Ham, Darlington and Motherwell. In Shanghai, Foochow and Bangkok.

All over the world — in Kiev, Killarney, Khartoum and Tashkent, in Quito, Quebec, Cairo and Cadiz — there were jack-o'-lanterns being carved. There were pumpkin pies baking and muffins muffining.

Now the trucks and boats and airplanes and carpets,
emptied of pumpkins, returned to the man, carrying
dollars.

He had enough money to buy the field.
And he had some extra, which he used to buy new
furniture to replace what he had sold.

But he didn't replace the paintings, because he had the field to look at.

And he didn't replace the watch, because he had the sun and the stars to tell him when it was day and when it was night.

The man might have planted more pumpkins. He had
kept one back for seeds. Pumpkins would make him rich.
But he had everything he needed.
So he decided to give the seeds away.

Because somewhere, someone might love another field pumpkins could save.